What If I Can't Explain God?

by Jennifer Grant

illustrated by Hsulynn Pang

beaming books

MINNEAPOLIS

God is hard to explain.

I've tried asking grown-ups to explain God, but
they aren't very good at it.

When they talk about God,
sometimes they say words like "outside of time"
or "everywhere all at once."
They say "Trinity" and "one in three, three in one."

I don't get it!
I ask again, and they shrug and say
God is hard to explain,
but I already know *that*.

I can't explain why I can't see God, even though sometimes God feels as close as my cat or the crayon in my hand when I'm coloring.

God nearby makes me feel happy and peaceful.

A lot of other things are hard for me to explain too . . .

Like how fizzy drinks tickle my nose and make me want to laugh and sneeze at the same time.

Or how dolphins have beaks and blowholes and live deep down in the ocean, but they want to be friends with *people*!

Or how, as soon as I was born, my parents knew it was really me, even though they had never even seen me before.

It's hard to explain why people all over the world speak all kinds of languages and say the exact same things!

And that's not all . . .
How can I explain what the sun is?

It's a *color*, yellow, a huge round ball in the sky,
but it's also a *feeling* and it warms my skin . . .
but it's *also light*.

When the sun comes up in the sky every day, it makes the morning happen, and sometimes I have to squint my eyes because it's so bright.

(And also, the sun is so far away that no one has ever even been there before!)

It's hard for me to explain my family too. My grandparents are "Nana" and "Papa," but my mom and dad call *them* "Mom" and "Dad," and my grandparents call each other "Sweetie" and "Honey."

A few days ago, I heard my nana call my mom "Baby," even though she's a grown-up!

But God is hardest of all to explain.

If God is more than one person,
like grown-ups say "three in one, one in three" . . .
then God is "they."

Maybe like fizzy drinks, they make us want to laugh
and sneeze at the same time.

Maybe, like dolphins, they are very different from us,
but they want to be friends with us.

Maybe they knew us before they even met us.

Maybe they say the same things in all different languages.

Maybe, like the sun, they warm and brighten and shine, all at the same time.

Maybe, like my grandparents, they have different names depending on who they're talking to.

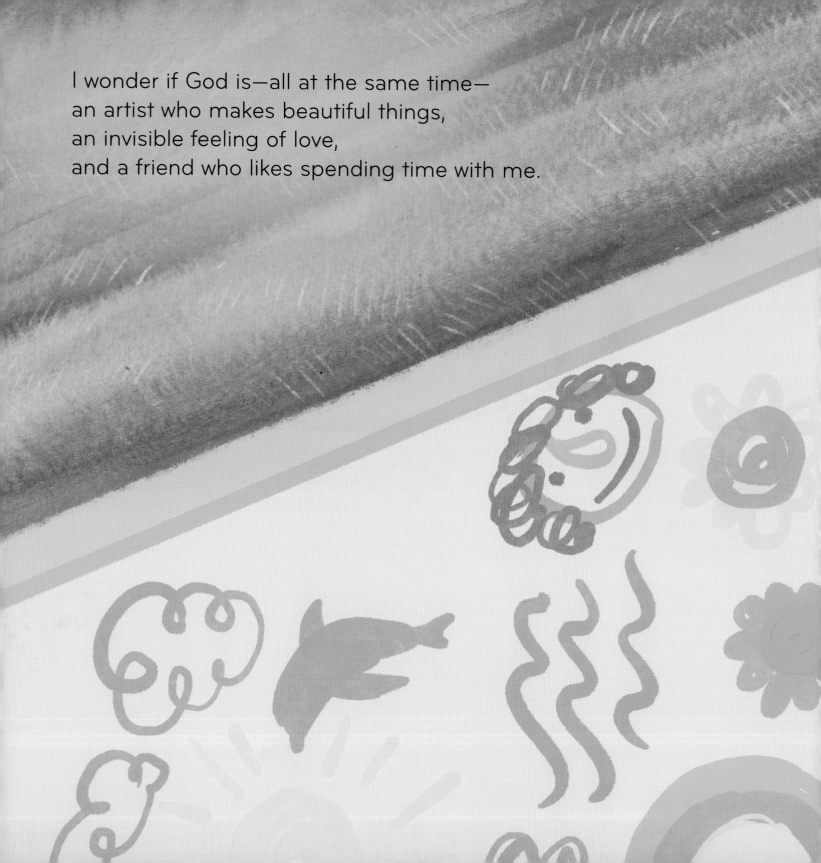

I wonder if God is—all at the same time—
an artist who makes beautiful things,
an invisible feeling of love,
and a friend who likes spending time with me.

Maybe all that matters is
knowing that God made me,
knowing that God is near me,
and knowing that God loves me.

Maybe it doesn't matter
if I can't explain God.

(Or that grown-ups can't either!)

For Matthias and Eleanor, with love
—JG

Text copyright © 2023 Jennifer Grant
Illustrations by Hsulynn Pang, copyright © 2023 Beaming Books

Published in 2023 by Beaming Books, an imprint of 1517 Media.
Printed in China.

29 28 27 26 25 24 23   1 2 3 4 5 6 7 8 9

Hardcover ISBN: 978-1-5064-8304-7
eBook ISBN: 978-1-5064-8305-4

Library of Congress Cataloging-in-Publication Data

Names: Grant, Jennifer (Jennifer C.), author. | Pang, Hsulynn, illustrator.
Title: What if I can't explain God? / by Jennifer Grant ; illustrated by
   Hsulynn Pang.
Other titles: What if I can not explain God?
Description: Minneapolis, MN : Beaming Books, 2023. | Audience: Ages 4-7. |
   Summary: A little girl reflects on the difficulty of explaining God,
   even for grownups, but concludes that maybe it does not matter if she
   can not put the nature of God into words.
Identifiers: LCCN 2022051810 (print) | LCCN 2022051811 (ebook) | ISBN
   9781506483047 (hardcover) | ISBN 9781506483054 (ebook)
Subjects: LCSH: God--Juvenile literature. | Faith--Juvenile literature.
Classification: LCC BT107 .G73 2023 (print) | LCC BT107 (ebook) | DDC
   231--dc23/eng/20230321
LC record available at https://lccn.loc.gov/2022051810
LC ebook record available at https://lccn.loc.gov/2022051811

Beaming Books
PO Box 1209
Minneapolis, MN 55440-1209
Beamingbooks.com

JENNIFER GRANT is the award-winning author of picture books for children and books for adults. Her books include *Maybe God Is Like That Too*, *Maybe I Can Love My Neighbor Too*, and *Dimming the Day*. Grant's work has appeared in *Woman's Day*, Chicago Parent, Patheos, and *Chicago Tribune*. Grant holds a master's degree in English literature with concentrations in creative writing and critical theory from Southern Methodist University in Dallas. A lifelong Episcopalian and mother of four, she lives in Chicago with her husband.

HSULYNN PANG is a Malaysian illustrator who enjoyed much of her childhood chasing after locusts and butterflies in her backyard, digging for earthworms and collecting seashells from the beach nearby. This is quite possibly why she finds herself painting lots of nature-inspired artworks. In addition to *What If I Can't Explain God?*, Hsulynn also illustrated *Gardens Are for Growing* by Chelsea Tornetto (Familius, 2022) and Grow (Clarion Books, 2021).